Printed in Hong Kong.

First U.S. edition   1   2   3   4   5   6   7   8   9   10

Library of Congress Cataloging in Publication Data
Baker, Alan. Benjamin's balloon / by Alan Baker.
p.   cm.   Summary: Benjamin blows up a balloon and begins a
travel adventure that causes him a certain amount of worry.
ISBN 0-688-09744-8.
[1. Hamsters—Fiction.]   I. Title.
PZ7.B1688Bf   1990   [E]—dc20
89-45897 CIP AC

Benjamin's Balloon

Story and pictures by

ALAN BAKER

Lothrop, Lee & Shepard Books
New York

Blowing up balloons
makes me nervous.

Oh, well. Here goes!

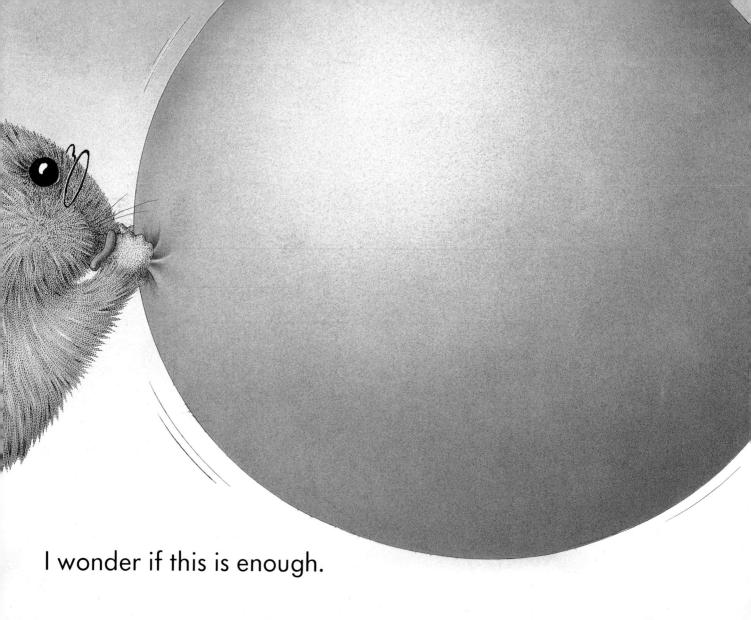

I wonder if this is enough.

Whoops. Maybe it's too much.
Hang on — going up!

Oh, dear. I don't like heights . . .

especially now that the air's
escaping.

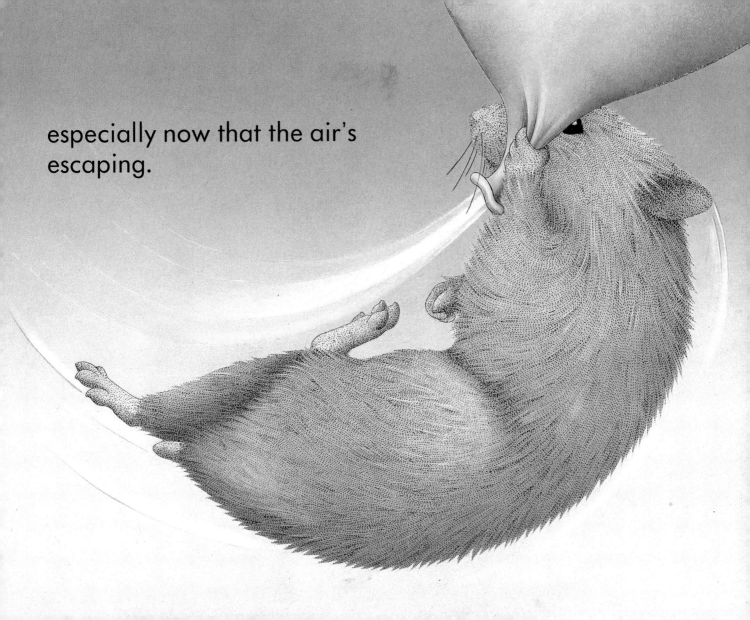

Snow! My fur will get all wet.

I hate wet fur.

The snow is coming down fast now.

And so am I.
Hope I don't land too hard.

At least the snow softened my fall.

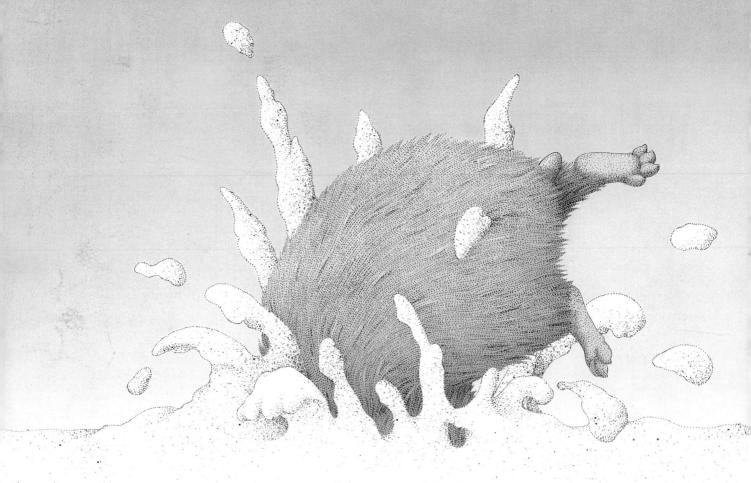

Hmmm . . . What else might snow be
good for?

I know! I can use it . . .

to get home.

That looks sturdy. Nice strong wings.
Smooth it over and . . .

climb aboard.

I've never liked flying.

But this way I'll get home fast.

Maybe *too* fast.

Not a bad landing, for a beginner.

I'm on the ground at last!

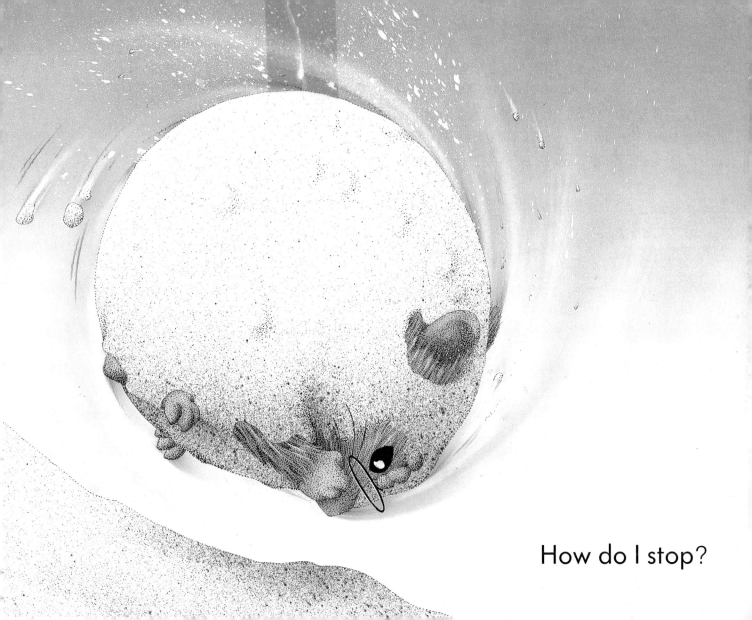

How do I stop?

Airborne again? I can't believe it.

Where am I?

Back where I started.
Enough traveling, I think.

Time to use my talents . . .

for something really worthwhile.